Grandma Rita lives in retirement in a Norfolk seaside village. She is married to Grandad Bill and has a little black cat called Samma. She is a part-time Lay Minister in the Church of England and her hobbies include gardening and family history. She likes to watch the sea and also writes poetry.

RITA BURGESS

Grandma's Water Tower Tales

AUSTIN MACAULEY PUBLISHERS™
LONDON * CAMBRIDGE * NEW YORK * SHARJAH

A CIP catalogue record for this title is available from the British Library.

ISBN 9781788230599 (Paperback)
ISBN 9781788230605 (E-Book)

www.austinmacauley.com

First Published (2018)
Austin Macauley Publishers™ Ltd.
25 Canada Square
Canary Wharf
London
E14 5LQ

I dedicate these stories to all my grandchildren.

My thanks goes to my husband, Bill, for his patience and encouragement.

Once upon a time, there was a Water Tower who lived by the sea whose name was Wat. His real name was WT but people called him Watty, for short. He was made of strong, white concrete and was extremely tall and wore a very long ladder at his side. He had lots of legs and because he was higher than anything else in his village, he could see right across all the rooftops to the sea. He sometimes felt he was guarding his village and liked to help whenever he could. But he did get lonely sometimes, as he did not have many friends.

One day, Watty said to himself, "I'm tired of just standing up here all day doing nothing but collecting water – I wish I could have some adventures." Watty liked having adventures; it usually meant he was able to help somebody somehow. Just then, Watty heard his neighbour, Farmer Rowe, start up his tractor. Trevor tractor lived in a huge black barn right next to Watty, and although they were sort of friends, they didn't speak much because Watty was too tall to hear what Trevor said. But today, Watty thought there was something different about Trevor. He often had a square trailer behind him to carry bales of hay, but today he was pulling a large, brown, oblong tank on wheels instead.

"What's going on?" wondered Watty, and just then Farmer Rowe shouted up very loudly, "Don't worry, Watty, we're just going to pump some of your water into Billy Bowser here to take across to the farm. A mains water pipe in the lane from the village has broken and we have no water to give the animals a drink."

Watty was so pleased he was able to help the animals – he had often seen them far below and wished he could get to know them better. There were cows and sheep, some pigs and a huge cart horse, as well as lots of geese and hens.

"That's all right," replied Watty. "I have plenty of water for you to take."

So the pumping began, and soon Billy Bowser was full right up. The farmer climbed up onto Trevor and very slowly the tractor pulled Billy, with his precious load of water, down the lane to the farm. Watty watched with excitement – he was going to be helpful to somebody today! First of all, Farmer Rowe asked Billy to give some water to the geese and chickens who were making quite a noise, rushing around in an agitated group. "Thanks, Billy," hissed the geese, "we can have a good wash now."

"Yes, thanks, Billy," squawked the chickens, "we need a drink." Then Trevor pulled Billy along the lane a bit further until they reached the fields where the cows and sheep lived. Farmer Rowe pumped water from Billy's long pipe into their drinking troughs.

"Thank you very much," bleated the sheep.

"Yes, thank you, thank you," mooed the cows.

"Now then, Trevor, just the pigs and then we're finished," said Farmer Rowe.

"Oh but what about Cory Carthorse?" asked Trevor.

"Yes of course," chuckled the farmer. "How could I have forgotten him?" So off they went, Trevor pulling Billy to the pig sties.

"Smashing, thanks a lot, Billy," grunted the pigs – and straight away lay down to wallow in the water.

"Watch out," shouted Trevor, "you're splashing it all over me! Don't waste the water or Watty won't like it." Finally, Trevor and Billy returned to the farmyard and stopped at the stables.

Cory Carthorse was really pleased to see them and the farmer gave him the last of Watty's water. "Thank you very much," neighed Cory, "it's a good thing we have Watty to give us his water in an emergency."

"Yes," said Farmer Rowe, "Watty has certainly done his good deed for the day."

That night, Watty looked out over the farm far below. "What an adventure I had today," he murmured to himself. "It's made me very happy knowing all those animals were able to have their drinks of water." Then a very weary Watty closed his eyes and was soon fast asleep.

Watty liked to help whenever he could. And one day, very early in the morning when he was just waking up, Watty thought he heard a shout from down the lane near the big black barn where Trevor tractor lived.

"Hello, what's up now?" thought Watty. Then he felt someone begin to climb his ladder. Soon a round, chubby face appeared, followed by a round, chubby little body in a bright green coat.

"Good morning, who are you?" asked Watty politely – he didn't like strangers clambering all over him without asking. Puffing loudly and breathing rather hard, the chubby little man introduced himself, raising his black bowler hat.

"My name is Horatio Tapp, I am the new head of the Water Company and I'm visiting every Water Tower to say hello and to see how you are getting on."

Watty was impressed. This was the very first time an official of the Water Company – which always insisted on capital letters in its name – had paid him a visit.

"I'm very pleased to meet you, sir," replied Watty. "I get along just fine and always try to help people when they need my water."

"That's the spirit," said Mr Tapp. "I thought I could rely on you, so I have a little job for you."

Watty was excited. Fancy a Water Company official needing his help, he thought. "I will always do what I can sir," he said.

"Well, it's like this," began Mr Horatio Tapp. "You know we haven't had any rain for ages?"

"Oh yes," replied Watty, "but I've got plenty saved up."

"Good," said Mr Horatio Tapp. "The problem is the Golf Club just down the road near the village is having a special Tournament next week but the greens are not green – they are all brown because it hasn't rained lately, and the Tournament may have to be cancelled. What you could do, Watty, is to let them have some of your water so the grass can have a long drink and go back to being green again. Then the VIPs will enjoy their weekend's golf and go home happy."

Watty had no idea what a Tournament was, but he had heard of VIPs and knew they were Very Important People who needed to go home happy! "No problem," he replied. "But how will you get the water all the way there?"

"Leave that to me," said Mr Horatio Tapp, "I know Billy Bowser, he'll be glad to help." Mr Tapp lowered himself carefully onto the rungs of Watty's long ladder. "Goodbye Watty, glad to have met you, and good luck with the golf course," he shouted.

"Goodbye, and thank you," yelled Watty, "I will do my very best."

Later that morning, Watty saw Trevor tractor coming down the lane with Billy Bowser close behind. "Have you come to help?" boomed Watty.

"Yes, Mr Horatio Tapp from the Water Company said we could have some of your water to take to the golf course," replied Trevor.

"Yes indeed," replied Watty, "Just ask someone to put on the hoses to pump my water over to you."

"But there's no one about," cried Billy. Just then a little boy whose name was Miles came round the corner of the lane riding his bright red bike.

"Ask Miles," shouted Watty, "I used to know his Grandma and I am sure he will know what to do."

Miles was very happy to help Watty and the others. His father was the farmer and had taught Miles how to do all sorts of useful things around the farm. When he saw the hefty hose which needed to connect Watty to Billy Bowser, Miles knew immediately what to do.

"Drive Billy over here, Trevor," instructed Miles, "then his tank will be near enough for me to connect the hose." So Trevor backed Billy up to the long, heavy hose and after several attempts, Miles managed to join Billy Bowser up to Watty. "Now turn on my water outlet, Miles," urged Watty, and very soon, gallons of Watty's water were pumping across into Billy Bowser's tank.

"Well done, Miles," shouted Watty. "That's enough for now; you can turn the tap off." So Trevor and Billy waited for Farmer Rowe, who had been on the phone to the Water Company, then they all trundled off along the lane to the Golf Club with Watty's water.

The Secretary of the Golf Club was a very worried man, as he thought the Tournament would have to be cancelled. But when he saw Trevor and Billy coming along he was very relieved to have water for his greens. "Now our Tournament can go ahead," he said happily, "thanks to Watty and his friends."

That night, Watty looked out towards the Golf Club far below. "What an adventure I had today," he murmured. "It's made me very happy knowing that the water I had in my tanks saved the Golf Tournament. Now all the VIPs can go home happy, and I hope they come again." And Mr Horatio Tapp went to bed happy, too, because he'd made a new friend – Watty.

Watty was happiest having adventures. He didn't think of problems, only adventures, so he was very pleased one week when he remembered that sometimes the village's Fire Station had Training Days when new firemen learned how to hold their long, heavy hoses to spray water onto a fire in order to put it out.

"I wonder if their Training Day is coming soon," thought Watty. "It is usually held in August and it would be nice to watch them from right up here." Just then, Watty heard someone bellowing loudly from below. It was Chief Fire Officer Fred Fillup in his smart white car with red stripes. He was shouting very loudly and was getting quite red in the face.

"Watty, we need your help! We don't have enough water in our fire tender for our Training Day tomorrow; can you spare any for us please?"

Watty was delighted to help. "Of course," he shouted back. "Just bring your appliance alongside and fill it up from my outlet."

Fred was really pleased to have Watty's help, and began giving orders on his radio. Soon there was a large, red fire engine charging through the village and along the lane with its noisy siren going. But it didn't have a clanging bell, which was something Watty was looking forward to.

"Perhaps it's broken, I will have to ask Fred," thought Watty.

Fred quickly organised his crew so that soon the fire engine was full up with water from Watty. "Thanks Watty," the Fire Chief called up. "Don't forget to watch us tomorrow!"

The next day Watty was up early, ready to watch the new recruits at the Fire

Station learning to use the hoses. "I expect they're really, really heavy when the water rushes through them," said Watty to himself. Suddenly, in a corner of the station yard, some flames began to flicker, and soon there was quite a fire burning ready for the new fire crew to practise on.

"OK, let's begin," shouted Fred to the three recruits, who were all kitted out in their uniforms and helmets, face masks, gloves and boots. They looked very big, Watty thought, and a bit like robots or spacemen. The new firemen, whose names were Kat, Matt and Pat, stood behind one another ready to hold the hose, and Pat, who was in front, held the hose nozzle, pointing it at the fire.

"Are you ready?" asked Fred, and turned on the water from the fire engine. But Pat wasn't quite ready and let go of the hose just at the same time as gallons of water rushed headlong through the nozzle and out into the yard. Of course, under such pressure, which the new fire officers weren't used to, the hose fell onto the floor and snaked about, moving in all directions, while Matt and Kat ran around trying to pick it up and put out the fire. High up above the Fire Station, Watty couldn't help laughing to himself at all the goings on. Eventually, Fred turned off the water, by which time the yard was flooded, all the firemen had wet feet, the fire had gone out of its own accord, and the three recruits stood sheepishly in a line waiting for the Fire Chief to tell them off. But Fred wasn't really cross. He understood what had happened and told them they could try again another day.

"We can't lose any more of Watty's water today," he explained. "Otherwise there won't be enough for you to try again."

The next day, Fire Chief Fred organised his recruits and showed them again how to hold the hose firmly so that when the water came through under pressure, they could point it at the fire properly. Soon another fire was blazing in the corner of the station yard, this time Kat was in front holding the nozzle firmly with both hands, with Matt and Pat behind her helping to hold the heavy hose. When the water started, she pointed the nozzle steadily at the fire and after a few minutes, it died down. Then Matt and Pat took it in turns to hold the nozzle, eventually putting out the fire completely.

"That's much better," cried Fred proudly, "you are all proper fire officers now you can handle a hose properly."

The Fire Chief came to see Watty that evening when he was off duty. "Thanks for all your water, Watty," smiled Fred, "all my fire crew, including Kat – by the way, did you know Kat is a girl, short for Katherine – all my crew have now learned to use the hoses under pressure, and it was because we were able to use your water that we could have our Training Day."

Watty had not realised that underneath the heavy uniform and helmet of one of the 'firemen', there was a girl. "Fancy that," Watty said to himself, "it's nice to know that girls can do boys' jobs sometimes." It was only after Fred had gone home that Watty remembered he had forgotten to ask about the fire engine's bell! "Oh well," he murmured to himself as he got ready for bed, "there'll be another Training Day next year, I'll ask then."

One morning in September Watty woke up early again. It was such a beautiful day: the birds were singing loudly, the sky was blue and the sun shone over the whole village and the sea, making it sparkle. While he was looking out to sea to see if there were any boats, Watty heard a shout from below, and felt someone climbing up his long ladder.

"It's only me again Watty," shouted a familiar voice, and Mr Horatio Tapp from the Water Company appeared once again, in the same bright green coat and black bowler hat as before. He was rather out of breath. Watty wondered what this was all about; did the Water Company need his help again? "It's like this, Watty," began Mr Horatio Tapp. "The Water Company has had a request from the Local Education Authority to allow a school visit for an outing here to teach the children all about where their water comes from, and how a Water Tower works."

"My goodness," thought Watty, "that would be exciting – and it would be good to meet some more villagers." So Watty told Mr Horatio Tapp that he would be very pleased to see the local school for a visit during the new term.

"A week today then, Watty," exclaimed Mr Horatio Tapp as he began to climb down the ladder. "I will arrange it."

The next week, when the day of the visit came, Watty was so excited he could hardly wait!

23

At precisely 10 o'clock, a large coach appeared along the lane and came to park nearby. It seemed to Watty that the whole school had arrived, but Mr Horatio Tapp had explained that it would be only the top class from the village Junior School who would be allowed to come. Watty could also see three adults – teachers he supposed – and talking to them and waving his arms about was Mr Horatio Tapp. The children were split into groups with their teachers and Watty could see they each had a clipboard and pencil.

"They all look very keen," said Watty to himself. "I wonder if I will have to answer any questions."

While the groups sat down between Watty's long legs to listen to their teachers and to Mr Horatio Tapp, who was telling them how a Water Tower worked and giving them exercises to do, Watty tried to hear what was going on – he was really too tall, but he could see the children drawing pictures. Suddenly he felt someone begin to climb the rungs of his ladder again.

"Goodness, what's this?" wondered Watty, and he watched anxiously to see who would want to climb up so high when all the action was going on down below.

"It's me, I'm Stanley," said a timid voice, "I only wanted to climb right up here to show that there is something I can do – the other children all call me Silly

Stanley, as I'm no good at reading or sums and all that." Stanley seemed to run out of steam as he was trying to explain why he had climbed Watty's long ladder. Watty saw that he was very nearly crying.

"Well, you've certainly proved you have a good head for heights and were brave enough to climb up here," said Watty, "and if you find your school work hard, you must ask your teacher for help."

"Yes I know," said Stanley, "but I'm a bit slow and by the time I have put my hand up, someone else has got to the teacher first."

"Well, I think you should say to yourself that you will just keep on trying," said Watty, "and try to be a bit quicker in class."

"Thanks, Watty," said Stanley, "it's good to have someone on my side, and thank you for not minding that I climbed up your ladder – you have a wonderful view up here by the way – and you can see my school." he added. All of a sudden there was a loud, frightened cry from below, from about halfway down Watty's ladder. Stanley looked over the edge. "Oh Watty," he exclaimed, "that boy who is always pushing in and showing off in class – Dennis his name is – has tried to follow me up your ladder, Watty, but he has turned a funny shade of green and is clinging onto the ladder and not moving." Watty shouted down,

"What's up, Dennis, are you all right?"

"No, I'm stuck," came a frightened voice, "I just can't move and I feel sick."

"Don't worry, I have someone up here who will help get you down," shouted Watty, looking across at Stanley.

"Yes of course," said Stanley, "I'm in the Cub Scouts and we must always be ready to help others." And before Watty could say any more, Stanley was quickly climbing back down the ladder. About halfway down, when he reached Dennis, Stanley managed to squeeze past him on the ladder so he was on the rung below. "Now then, Dennis," said Stanley, "I'm right here, and I will hold your ankles and guide your feet down, step by step."

So very slowly, with Stanley guiding him, Dennis was able to descend Watty's long ladder and reach the safety of the ground.

"Are you all right?" boomed Watty as the two boys re-joined their classmates.

"Yes thank you Watty," shouted Dennis, "Stanley was so brave, I could never have climbed down without him, and he must be really special to be able to climb right to the top of your long ladder."

Watty smiled to himself. Now perhaps the children would respect Stanley a bit more and not call him silly. Watty watched as the children finished their lesson underneath his legs, and went back onto their coach. As they went they all looked up and shouted as loudly as they could, "Three cheers for Watty!"

"Well," Watty thought, as he looked across the village to the school. "I've met some new folk today, a whole classful! And those two special boys, Stanley and Dennis. I do hope they will come and visit me again."

That night, before he went to sleep, Watty thought how lucky he was that he had made some new friends, but he did wonder, with all the excitement, why nobody had asked him any questions about water towers.

Watty did get lonely sometimes, but he did like having adventures. The weather soon began to turn very cold and Watty began to think he would not see the friends he had made from school. But one day in winter Watty woke up to a big surprise. Everything around him was white: the village and fields and woods and lanes were all covered in snow! And it was very, very cold. The snow had drifted up all along the lane and hedges, and Watty wondered if his friends were all right.

"It must be very difficult walking in all that soft stuff," he said to himself, "I wonder if the school will be open." Just then Watty spotted Farmer Rowe's son, Miles, coming round the corner of the lane, pulling what looked like a large tray on a rope.

"Hello, Watty," shouted Miles loudly, so that Watty could hear – sometimes they didn't speak much because Watty was too tall to hear what Miles said. "Are you all right in this weather?"

"Yes thanks," replied Watty, "but my legs and feet are a bit cold." Miles laughed. "Yes, I can see you don't have any boots on like me," he said. "And I'm wearing my scarf and hat, and the mittens which Grandma knitted me last Christmas, so I'm as warm as toast."

Watty was puzzled about the tray. "Where are you going?" he shouted as Miles went across the lane to the cottage next door.

"We have a day off school today because of the snow, so I'm calling for my friend Anthony and his brother Elliot to go sledging," shouted Miles. And he plodded up the path to the house where his friends lived, and knocked. The door opened very quickly, and two small boys tumbled out, both wrapped up

warmly with woolly hats and scarves and gloves, and just like Miles they were pulling trays too!

Again Watty was puzzled. "I don't know a game called sledging," he boomed, "How do you play it?"

Miles laughed again. "Well, it's not really a game, but it's a lot of fun and we can only do it when we have snow – that's why we've brought our sledges, we thought we would go up to the top field where there's a bit of a hill," he said. "Just watch, Watty, and you will see what I mean."

So Miles and his friends went off up the lane, kicking up the snow as they went and stamping along until they reached the gate to the top field. But when they tried to open the gate, it was stuck fast, frozen, with the snow drifted up against it. "Oh well, we'll just have to use the lane for sledging," suggested Elliot, "It's not as steep as the field but it does have a bit of a hill." So the boys lined up one behind the other, sat down on their sledges and grasped the ropes. Then one by one off they went, sliding and skidding down the lane right back down to Watty.

"That does look fun," boomed Watty, "can you do it again?"

"Rather!" shouted Miles. So they all tramped back up the lane pulling their sledges, and when they reached the top off they went again – whoosh, whoosh, whoosh – faster this time because their sledges had made a track in the snow to make it slippery. And they did this lots and lots of times, till their faces were glowing and they felt all warm inside.

Then Watty called out again, "What about building a snowman, boys – it would give me someone to talk to." So excited were the boys, they quickly stacked

their sledges up against Watty's long ladder and began picking up handfuls of snow. Soon there was a large round mound, then a smaller one on top out in the lane. "You need to give him a mouth and two eyes and a nose," shouted Watty, "otherwise he won't be able to talk to me."

"I'll just pop along and ask my dad for something to make his face," said Elliot, and soon he came back carrying some pieces of coal, a large carrot and an old pipe – and a very long multi-coloured scarf Grandma had knitted years ago which nobody wanted to wear. "We'll soon have him shipshape, then you can have a chat with him, Watty," said Miles, smiling. And within moments, the snowman had two eyes, a long orange nose, and looked as if he was smoking a pipe in his mouth. He appeared to be nice and warm with his scarf wound around his neck too. The boys then dug around in the snow and found two long pieces of twig for the snowman's arms.

"Well done, boys, now I will have someone to talk to when you've all gone home," said Watty, "but what about his head, he needs a hat."

"Thanks Watty, that's a good idea, we'll see if we can find an old one indoors, but what can we do about your cold feet?" asked Anthony.

"I know," said Elliot, "why don't we ask the Cubs from the Scout Hut in the village, I'm sure they would like to help."

So Elliot, Miles and Anthony went slithering and sliding back down the lane to the village to the hut where the Scouts and Guides had their meetings. Luckily some of them were there getting ready to go out and help clear snow from people's paths. When Elliot explained how cold Watty was in the snow, and that they needed a hat for the snowman, the Scouts said, "Leave it to us,

we're always ready to help." The boys clambered as fast as they could along the snowy road back to Watty. "Watty, I think you are going to have warm legs soon," shouted Elliot, "and maybe the snowman might have a hat to keep him warm too."

Just then, Watty saw a long line of boys and girls plodding along the lane in their boots and gloves and anoraks. "Hello, Watty, we heard your legs and feet were cold in this snow, so we have come to help," said the tallest girl, whose name was Rosie. "Come along, Cubs, get to it." And suddenly Watty felt three pairs of arms go round each of his six legs as the boys and girls cuddled up to Watty and hugged him, as they held tightly to each other.

"Oh, that's lovely," boomed Watty, "Thank you all very, very much. My legs feel much warmer now." Then he realised that some of the children hugging him were the same ones who had come to learn all about water towers back in the autumn. Watty was so thrilled to see Stanley again. "Well done, Stanley, thank you very much," cried Watty as he began to feel warmer. Then Stanley delved into one of his pockets and pulled out a bright red woolly hat.

"Will this do for your snowman?" he asked.

"Oh yes, thank you," cried Elliot, "Now he really looks properly dressed for this wintry weather."

Miles, Anthony and Elliot had to go back for their tea, and the other children needed to go off helping to clear the snow. Then somehow, no one knew quite how because it was so magical, the snowman had begun to move. One minute he was out in the lane, the next he had come right up underneath Watty. So Watty and the snowman had a nice long chat, although the snowman didn't

say much, just listened, or perhaps Watty couldn't hear him very well because he was so high up. But all in all, Watty told the snowman, he felt very lucky, because not many water towers could say they had lots of friends. Watty told the snowman how he liked to have adventures and that was how he had made friends at the same time. Watty thought perhaps the snowman was a bit timid, as he didn't have much to talk about, but in fact after a few hours, when Watty went to say goodnight to him, he had gone away, leaving behind just a red woolly hat and a very long woolly scarf.

That night, looking out over the silent, sleeping village, Watty thought how lucky he was that he had made so many new friends this year through having adventures.

"I wonder what next year will bring," he thought as he settled down to sleep.